the
LOVERS

THE TAROT
TRILOGY
BOOK THREE

J.D. BRETTON

THE LOVERS

THE TAROT TRILOGY, BOOK THREE

J.D. Bretton

Printed in the United States of America

First Printing August, 2018

Splintered Sky Publishing

ISBN: 9780997468274 (Print)
ISBN: 9780997468267 (eBook)

Cover Design by Fiona Jayde
Interior Design by The Deliberate Page

For L.S.-
For being the first reader

*Our destiny is frequently met in the
very paths we take to avoid it.*

Jean de La Fontaine

CHAPTER 1

The screen door slammed.

"I'll be right out," Danielle yelled from the back room. She covered her paints and quickly rinsed off her brushes. Glancing in the mirror, she wiped a smudge of blue from her cheek and attempted to smooth her unruly curls. She and Sawyer had made plans for drinks and dinner over at the Playa Bar. If he was going to come early, this was as good as it was going to get.

"You know, you weren't supposed to be here until six." When she entered the front room, it was not Sawyer who greeted her. A man held one of her paintings. The wing tattoo on his neck hit her like a blow to the chest. She touched her shoulder where her own recently etched tattoo was placed. "Can I help you?"

The man's back tensed before he turned.

"Danielle."

It was only one word, but in it she heard an inexplicable mix of longing and pain.

"Do I know you?" Danielle wrinkled her forehead.

The man smiled, but his eyes remained sad. He was tall and lanky, his skin a light brown. In jeans and a t-shirt, he looked out of place for the beach. Danielle recognized him as the man she had seen a few weeks ago at the Playa Bar.

"No, your name is on your business cards on the counter. I'm Noah, Noah Hunt."

His voice was low and deep, and melted in her ears until she could almost taste its velvety sweetness. He extended his hand. A jolt of energy coursed through her palm when they touched. His skin was rough and callused, his grip strong, yet gentle. Her heart pounded.

"It's good to see you. Good to meet you, I mean." His eyes fell to the long, red scar on her shin. "What happened to your leg?"

"Just a paddleboarding accident." Danielle pulled her hand back. "Is there something I can do for you?"

"I was checking out your paintings. You're really talented. I didn't know you could paint like that, that someone could paint like that, on driftwood, with paint." Noah exhaled and ran his fingers over his closely cropped hair. He shifted from foot to foot.

Danielle peered uneasily at Noah.

"I'm new in town and looking for work. I'm a photographer. I was wondering if I could rent a spot in your store to sell my pictures."

"Did you bring a portfolio with you?" Danielle crossed her arms.

"Um...no. I figured I'd talk to you first." Noah placed the driftwood back on the display shelf.

"Can you come back with your pictures? I'd need to see your work first. Do you live in Areto?"

"Yeah, I have a place not too far away on the beach."

"Well, stop back and I'll take a look." Danielle couldn't shake the feeling that she knew him. She rummaged on the counter for one of her business cards.

"Nice tattoo that you've got, by the way. Why the wing?" Noah asked.

"It reminds me of someone I used to know. What about you? I saw you have a wing too." *Not that I'm staring at your beautiful body.*

"A reminder to dream, rise above limitations."

Those words. She shivered. It seemed a lifetime ago when she heard those exact words from Xavier's lips. She pictured him on the kitchen counter, jeans slung low on his hips. Danielle turned. Noah stepped toward her. His dark eyes drew her in.

The screen door squeaked and jarred her out of her reverie. Sawyer bounded into the store with sandy feet and swim trunks, his long blonde hair pulled back in a ponytail.

"Ready for a beautiful sunset and drinks at the Playa?"

"Sure," Danielle murmured, unable to take her eyes from Noah.

Sawyer put his arms around her.

"This is Noah Hunt. He just moved here. Noah, this is Sawyer Reed. He owns the surf shop."

As they shook hands, they sized each other up like two prizefighters.

"Nice to meet you." Noah shoved his hands into his pockets.

"You too. Aren't you a little overdressed for the beach?" Sawyer chided.

"I rode my bike here. You ever ride a bike?"

"Dude, you're in Areto. We ride the waves. That must be your bike I see parked by the horse ranch. Are you the guy living in the tent?"

Noah glared at Sawyer.

"For now. I'll see you soon, Danielle." Noah strode out. The door banged shut behind him.

"He left in a hurry."

Danielle raised her eyebrows. "You weren't exactly your charming self. What happened to being the Areto welcoming committee?"

"That was special for you."

"Yeah, right." Danielle laughed. "Me and all the other girls you tried to pick up."

"I didn't like the way he was looking at you. What did he want?" Sawyer pulled her tightly against his chest.

"Getting a little possessive, are you? He wanted to sell his photographs here."

"Be careful. He could be a weirdo. He does live in a tent."

"Yeah, maybe he snaps photographs of his victims before he buries them in the sand. Come on, let's go."

The light from the setting sun illuminated the brown sand in front of the Playa Bar. The beach sparkled as if it were frosted with a million tiny stars. The waves thundered, the sea alive, rolling toward Danielle. It dared her to enter. She ran her hands over the bumpy scar on her leg. Her paddleboarding mishap had only increased her trepidation toward the ocean.

Her life was filled with regrets, but ironically, almost drowning was not one of them. It marked a turning point when she was finally able to begin to let go of her past. The loss of her child, murder of her husband, and her affair with Xavier Hawthorne, a ghost, were memories that she could now lock away. They faded into the background, a quiet murmur that would never be silenced completely but no longer screamed at her every second of the day.

She had Sawyer to thank for that. She wasn't sure if it was love, but he was exactly what she needed. He sat next to her, one hand on her thigh. He chatted with whomever happened by and garnered more than a few appreciative gazes from the bikini-clad tourists. Sawyer was easy, fun, and uncomplicated — the complete opposite of her usual brooding melancholy.

As Danielle stared out at the water, thoughts of Noah seeped from the corners of her brain. She had seen him only once before, at the Playa Bar, but his face haunted her. So much so, she had drawn him in her sketchbook, attempting to discover why he seemed familiar.

"Hey, Danielle. Are you there?" Sawyer nudged her shoulder.

"Yeah, sorry. I was getting lost in the sunset."

"It is beautiful. Especially because I'm here with you."

"So smooth, do you have these lines written down in a book?"

Sawyer wrapped his arm around her waist. "You inspire me."

He leaned in for a kiss. As he pulled away, he trailed his hand down her belly to land in her lap.

"*Algo para tomar?*" asked the waitress.

"*Dos Medallas, por favor, y una orden de sorullitos.*"

"Beer and corn fritters. You sure know the way to a girl's heart."

A banana boat filled with screaming teenagers streamed past the bar.

"Look at this guy sitting in the beach chair, the one with the red bathing suit. He's got a tuft of cotton hanging out on the top of his dome. Dude needs to shave that off." Sawyer smirked.

"You're so mean, Goldilocks. Maybe his wife is turned on by his tuft."

"I'm only observing. Your turn."

It was a game they'd played when they first met. Danielle had been painting the mural at his shop when they started having lunch together upstairs in his apartment. Not much for conversation at that point, he entertained her with his running commentaries on the people passing by. He made her laugh, at a time when all she wanted to do was cry.

Danielle scanned the restaurant and sipped on her beer. Even though the sun was sinking, its heat warmed her cheeks. The tang of the cold beer refreshed her and complemented the sweet corn of the sorrulitos.

"See the guy with blue t-shirt over by the pool table. Looks like a big muscle head."

"Got him." Sawyer left his hand in her lap and slowly rubbed his thumb back and forth. The thin fabric of her sundress offered little protection from the sensation.

Danielle tried to keep her voice even and hoped the table concealed his actions.

"Wait until he turns around. He's totally got 80s girl jeans on."

"That seems a little sexist. Who's a mean girl now?"

"Oh, come on. They're bedazzled on the pockets."

"I might have a pair like that in my closet."

Sawyer increased the pressure of his thumb. Danielle's belly tightened. She gripped the edges of the table.

"You're such a tease, Sawyer Reed," she whispered.

"Just trying to keep you interested, Danielle Williams. Look at this one. Red dress coming up the beach. She looks like she's on a mission. Wouldn't want to be on the receiving end of that. What, no comments from the peanut gallery?"

"It's a little hard to concentrate right now."

Sawyer smirked. He steadied her with a tight grasp of her waist as he pressed into her clit, faster now. "And look, she's headed this way."

"She's very...pretty." Danielle's breath became rapid.

The woman's silky brown hair fell past her shoulders. Her long earrings glinted in the fading light. Her dress hugged her voluptuous curves.

"But look at her eyes, those are the crazy eyes. You stay away from that mess." Sawyer held her tighter as shudders coursed through her body. "I think we need a new game."

"That might be a good idea." Danielle looked around. In the noise and confusion of the bar no one paid any attention to them.

"Your place?"

Danielle smiled. "As long as you don't mind the cockroaches."

A necessary evil of island living, Danielle hadn't been able to control the population of mini-beasts that lurked in the cabinets and dark corners of her apartment. It was an uneasy arrangement, but one she was willing to endure for the gorgeous views and weather.

Sawyer took her hand and led her out of the bar. The wet sand squished under her feet; translucent crabs skittered away into their holes.

"You should call someone to spray your building. Talk to Ramón. I bet he'd take care of it for you. Especially since his little tryst with your mother."

"Ugh. Don't remind me of that. But I'll ask him." In typical style, when her mother Marla had visited, she'd hooked up with Danielle's landlord, Ramón.

Before she knew it, they arrived at the door of her shop. She fumbled with the key.

"Nervous?" Sawyer ran his hand across her back.

"No, I'm still recovering from the Playa." She stood on her toes to kiss him. Walking through the door, flashes of Noah and their brief interaction earlier popped into her head. She imagined what it would be like to kiss his soft, full lips, what it would feel like to have his hands pull her close. What was wrong with her? She shouldn't be fantasizing about a stranger with Sawyer right here beside her. She led Sawyer up the stairs directly to her bed.

"Getting right down to business tonight. Nice."

Danielle headed into the bathroom and returned with a condom.

"And prepared." Sawyer leaned back. "Ouch." He put his hands under his back and retrieved drawing pencils. "You're like a pack rat. What else have you got in here?" Sawyer ran his hand under the crumpled sheets. "A notebook, playing cards, crackers..."

"It's called a sketchbook, and tarot cards, and the crackers, well, they're just crackers. I like to have the things I need close by."

"And do I fall in to that category?"

"You are in bed with the crackers and the pencils, so I guess so."

"I think I should pick out a card." Sawyer opened the box and pulled out a card. "The Fool?" Sawyer frowned. "That's a terrible card. Although I am a fool for you."

Danielle rolled her eyes and threw the box to the side. "The Fool shows your happy-go-lucky ways. Shall I do the honors?" She waved the condom in the air.

As Sawyer wiggled out of his shorts, Danielle ripped open the package and climbed onto the bed. She straddled him and rolled the condom down his shaft. As she lowered herself, he groaned with pleasure. Sawyer wrapped his arms around her and they rose and fell with the sweet rhythm of the waves.

As Danielle rested her cheek on the pillow she came eye to eye with her sketchbook, the page opened to the picture of the man from the bar — Noah Hunt. He continued to haunt her thoughts. His intense eyes stared back at her, accusing. Inexplicable guilt crept over her. She stretched out her arm to flip over the sketchbook, then buried her face in Sawyer's hair. But as he arched inside her, it was not Sawyer she pictured in her mind, but Noah.

CHAPTER 2

Danielle fumbled in her bed to find her phone to silence the alarm. She threw off the sheet and pulled on her shorts and t-shirt from the crumpled heap on the floor. Since her accident, she had traded her late-night swims for dawn jogs on the beach before the heat of the day made it unbearable. Danielle laced on her sneakers and pondered her route. She usually ran past Sawyer's shop and the Playa bar to the town beach. She pulled her tarot cards from under her pillow and shuffled the deck.

"What's in store for me today?" She split the deck and turned over the top card. The Lovers. "Sawyer, I get it." Danielle muttered. "Well, I'm not listening." She decided to head the opposite way.

It had been a little awkward with Sawyer last night. Immediately after they made love, she had escaped into the shower. He left shortly after, saying he was going surfing early in the morning. She yawned and rubbed the sleep from her eyes as she stumbled down the stairs.

When she got outside, she headed left. She waved to the fishermen out in their boats as they dragged the water for bait. Her feet pounded a slow rhythm on the sand as she passed the small concrete houses that lined the beach. The salt of the breeze stung her skin. The palm trees arched overhead and swayed in the wind.

As she continued, the houses were spaced farther apart. Roosters crowed in a fenced-in yard. She squinted and saw a tent down the beach. It would be a greater distance than she usually ran, but curiosity got the better of her. As the brown tent grew closer, Danielle wondered if Noah was inside. She noticed a tiny access road behind the beach where a motorcycle was parked. She was only a couple yards away now. The tent flapped open and Noah exited, bare-chested. His dark skin glistened in the rising sun. When he glanced down the beach and saw Danielle, a smile spread across his face. This time the smile reached his eyes. How could he look at her like that, as if she was the most glorious sight in the world in her holey t-shirt and running shorts? It was a look that you would give a long-lost friend, not a person you barely knew. It made no sense.

"Nice morning for a run."

Danielle managed a nod and continued past him. She sensed his gaze on her back and her cheeks reddened. A short distance away the beach curved around an outcrop of trees and rock where she would be hidden from Noah's view. Danielle rounded the corner and stopped, bracing her hands on her knees to catch her breath. She usually ran her meager mile roundtrip, but she had probably already gone that far. Why hadn't she brought water? Maybe she could avoid going back past Noah by finding a way to the main road. She could walk back that way. It didn't seem likely since the beach was rocky and overgrown in this area, but it was worth a try.

She followed a trail that wound its way through the rocks. It ended on a ridge where a group of *flamboyán* trees formed a canopy of red flowers. Danielle sat in the shade and contemplated her long run, or walk, back home. Hopefully Noah would be gone. Why did it even matter? Noah Hunt was getting in her head in a bad way.

The heat of the sun and her thirst intensified by the minute, so she reluctantly followed the path back to the beach. As she rounded the corner, Noah sauntered out of the waves. The water dripped lusciously off his brown skin. When he saw her, his eyes locked with hers. She didn't turn away, trapped in the captivating depth of his dark eyes.

"It's getting hot out here."

"Yup." Sweat dripped down her forehead, neck, and pretty much everywhere else.

"I've got water in my tent. I'll get you a bottle."

"No, that's okay. I'm fine."

"It's not a problem, just wait a minute."

Noah ducked into his tent and returned with a bottle. As she reached to grab it, their fingers touched for the briefest moment. Her skin burned, nerves electrified.

"Thanks."

"Anytime." Noah grinned, revealing an adorable dimple in his left cheek.

As Danielle continued down the beach, she couldn't contain the slight smile that graced her own face.

Back in her apartment, she jumped into the shower. She toweled off, then flopped onto her bed picturing Noah, his dark skin shimmering as he got out of the water. This was going to be a problem. She rummaged through her sheets until she found her tarot cards. She shuffled the deck and pulled out a card — the Hanged Man. Danielle remembered what Vanessa had said about this card at her last reading. Change, transformation, something like that. Danielle needed guidance. Between Sawyer, her past with Xavier, and now Noah clouding the picture, a visit to Vanessa might be just what she needed. *It could be a little scary*, thought Danielle, *but what the hell*. Hopefully she wouldn't kiss her like she did at the group reading. Danielle chuckled. She slipped on shorts and a tank top and headed out the door.

The green concrete house was a short walk past the Playa Bar. A wooden sign propped outside advertised Messages from Beyond: medium, tarot readings, botanica. As Danielle pushed open the screen door, a bell attached to the hinges jangled.

The room was decorated simply. A single rectangular wooden table with four chairs took up most of the space in the center of the room. The walls were lined with shelves filled with candles, saints, and jars of herbs. Danielle perused the labels. There were candles that promised love, money, health, and protection from evil.

Vanessa Rivera came from behind a purple curtain that hung in the back doorway. Her straight dark hair hung past her shoulders. Tattoos of roses, skulls, and crosses covered her chest and shoulders.

"Danielle, *bienvenida*. I'm glad you decided to pay me a visit." Vanessa gestured for Danielle to sit. "What can I help you with today? A candle, some herbs, perhaps a tarot reading?

Danielle sat on her hands to keep them from shaking. "A tarot reading. I have a couple questions."

"*Claro que sí*. We'll do a Celtic Cross." Vanessa handed her the deck of tarot cards. "Shuffle the deck, *por favor*."

Danielle shuffled the cards and took a deep breath. She wasn't sure she was ready for this.

When she finished, Vanessa held her hands over Danielle's and the deck. "*Díme*, what question do you seek guidance on?" Vanessa stared at her with dark eyes rimmed with kohl.

"I need to figure out my love life. There's my complicated past, I'm seeing someone now, and I just met this other guy. I'm trying to sort everything out; it's kind of a mess."

"Let's find out what the cards tell us. Please cut the deck." Danielle divided the cards and Vanessa began to lay them on the table. "The first card is your present, the Lovers. And the second card, the Knight of Wands. Your two relationships. And in the past, the Three of Swords. The pain and sorrow of your past prevents you from moving forward and making a decision."

"Yeah, I've heard that before." It seemed like a lifetime since her reading with Nancy back in Fairview only three months ago.

Vanessa continued, "The Sun, this is what you hope to achieve. Family, children, a happy life. This will never happen, if you don't let go of your past and realize history does not always have to repeat itself. Interesting. The

Hanged Man looks over your shoulder. It speaks of transformation. You must be open to see this transformation for the truth that it is."

Danielle sighed; more riddles. Sawyer certainly hadn't changed, and she barely knew Noah. "But what do I do? How do I know what the right choice is to make?"

Vanessa turned another card. "Five of Cups. You have lost much, but you need to look beyond your losses to find your destiny, the love that you know is true. *Mira.* Look. The Chariot and Strength cards. You possess great strength and courage. Do not be afraid. You will make the right choice."

Danielle hoped that Vanessa was right. But who was the right choice: Sawyer? Noah?

Vanessa placed the last two cards on the table. "Death and the Ten of Cups."

Danielle touched the Ten of Cups card. The happy coupled embraced. Their two children danced next to them. It was all that she ever wanted.

"If you can accept change, you will achieve what you desire."

"Thanks, Vanessa. I hope you're right."

"You have everything you need, Danielle. Open your eyes to what is right there in front of you. *Ahora tengo una pregunta para tí.*" Vanessa tapped her pointed fingernails against the table.

Oh no, thought Danielle, *she's going to ask me about the kiss.*

"How long have you been seeing ghosts?"

"What? I don't see ghosts."

"This man from your past, *es un fantasma, verdad*?"

"Why would you say that?" Danielle bit her lip.

Vanessa shook her head. "Let's be truthful with each other, *sí*? The night you came to the reading, your ghost paid you a visit through me. You have a strong connection to the spirit world."

Danielle got up and knocked her chair over in the process. She picked it up and pulled money from her pocket. "I've got to go."

"How long will you run, Danielle? You can't push this part of yourself aside forever and hide it from others. Embrace who you are, or you will never be happy."

Danielle placed the money on the table and rushed out the door. Vanessa's throaty laugh echoed behind her.

Danielle folded and taped brown paper around the picture and placed it in a bag for the customer.

"I hope you enjoy it."

"I'm going to hang it right over my desk at work, so I can remember this vacation when I'm freezing my ass off and I'm ready to pull my hair out. You're lucky to be able to live here."

"Yes, I am," Danielle realized as she agreed. Her dark past, the losses behind her, she was able to pursue her art, and she had Sawyer. She should embrace what was right in front of her. Maybe she could be happy with Sawyer, make a life here.

As the customer left, another woman pushed past her through the door. She crossed her arms and pursed her lips together, frowning.

Danielle recognized her as the woman in the red dress from the other night at the Playa. She recalled Sawyer's warning about her crazy eyes.

"Can I help you?"

"Are you Danielle?" The woman uncrossed her arms and balled her hands into fists.

"Yes." Danielle suddenly felt this was the wrong answer.

"Where is he? Is he here?"

"Where is who?" Danielle immediately pictured Sawyer. Was this one of his previous conquests with a possessive streak?

"Noah, that bastard. Is he here? Is he upstairs?"

"Noah, Noah Hunt?"

"Yeah, bitch. Noah Hunt." The woman slammed one hand on the counter and shoved the other in Danielle's face. "See this? It's an engagement ring."

Danielle put up her hands. "Listen, I don't know him. He came in to the store once wanting to sell his photographs."

"Sell his photographs?" The woman air quoted the final word. "Photographs?" Her voice escalated into a high pitch. "Noah works construction. He isn't a fucking photographer. Where is he? Don't think I won't come behind that counter and mess you up. I came all the way from Fairview. I'm not leaving until I get my hands on him."

"Fairview? You're from Fairview? I used to live there." Danielle's eyes widened.

"Oh, honey, you are digging yourself a bigger and bigger hole. How long have you been the side chick?"

"Side chick? I'm not anybody's side chick."

"Then explain to me why after his motorcycle accident when he nearly died on that road, while he's half out of it with drugs—Danielle, Danielle, that's the only thing I hear for three fucking days. Then he checks himself out of the hospital and disappears. And ends up here…with you…Danielle."

"I swear I don't know him." Danielle noticed her sketchbook next to her on the counter opened to the picture of Noah. She prayed that the woman would not look down. She needed to get her out of here fast.

"I think he's living in a tent on the beach. That way." Danielle pointed. She felt a little sorry for selling Noah out.

"So now you know where he lives?" The woman narrowed her eyes.

"Areto's a small town. Everyone knows each other." Danielle backed away from the counter.

The woman reached out and grabbed Danielle's arm.

"I'm not finished with you yet." She glanced at the counter and picked up Danielle's sketchbook with her other hand. "What the hell? This is Noah. You bitch. I am going to fuck you up."

Danielle put her one free hand in front of her face.

"Hold on. Let's talk about this. I draw lots of people in town," Danielle rambled.

At that moment Sawyer tramped in, wet and sandy from a day of surfing.

"What's going on, ladies?"

The woman glared at Danielle as she released her arm. "This isn't over. And if you see that asshole, tell him Kira was here." She stormed out slamming the door behind her.

"What was that about?" Sawyer raised his eyebrows and whistled.

"I'm not sure." Danielle's whole body trembled. "That guy who lives in the tent, Noah, she's his fiancée, I guess. She thinks I know him for some reason."

"That's the woman from Playa the other night. I told you she had crazy eyes. You just attract trouble."

"It was strange. She said they live in Fairview. He was in a motorcycle accident."

Sawyer came behind the counter and put his arm around her.

"It'll be okay. Do you want to hang out tonight? I can protect you from any other insane women who decide to accost you."

"I'm actually kind of tired. I think I'm just going to go to bed early."

Sawyer picked up her sketchbook from the counter.

"This is Noah. You're drawing pictures of him?"

"I draw lots of things. It's not a big deal." Danielle shrugged.

"Yeah, you're right. It's no big deal." Sawyer put his hands on her shoulders and kissed her on the cheek. "If you need me, you know where to find me."

"Sawyer, wait…" Danielle sighed as he walked out, but she didn't follow.

Danielle puttered around the store and mulled over the day's events. She locked the door, not wanting any more unexpected visitors, and went to her back room to organize her supplies. Cleaning always helped her think. Maybe she should have gone after Sawyer. The sketch she did of Noah bothered him. But more importantly, why did she draw it in the first place? And that woman, what the hell? She was nuts.

She picked up a crumpled paper from the floor and unfolded it. It was a sketch of the dream she had shortly after she arrived in Areto. The rainy night, the motorcycle skidding across the pavement in front of her house in Fairview, the lightning. At times, her dreams came true. Was this the accident that Kira had told her about? Questions bubbled up inside her. Why would Noah have come here? Why did he say her name at the hospital? The face in the drawing stared back at her with Noah's eyes, eyes that somehow reminded her of Xavier.

Danielle shook her head. *I can't keep getting sucked into the past. Dreams are only dreams no matter what Vanessa says.* Danielle threw the picture in the trash and trudged upstairs to bed.

She hesitated before turning the handle. No lights shined from within the house. She pushed open the door and walked in darkness, pausing at the entrance to the living room. She knew the exact spot where Matt laid on the floor, where his blood flowed onto her hands when he died in her arms.

"It took you long enough to come. He's been waiting."

A child with golden curls hopped on one foot in the hallway.

"Come play with me." The girl ran up the stairs.

Danielle followed as she disappeared around the corner. When Danielle got to the top of the stairs, she turned to her bedroom, the place where she had torn herself from Xavier's final embrace. She opened the door and stepped onto the beach in Areto. The moonlight glittered on the waves. Xavier stood by the water.

She ran to him and wrapped her arms around his waist.

"*Where have you been? I've been looking for you,*" Xavier whispered.

"*I don't know how to find you anymore. It's been so confusing. I miss you.*"

"*I know, but I'm here now. Kiss me.*"

Danielle closed her eyes and kissed him deeply. When she opened her eyes, it was not Xavier's face, but Noah's that she saw.

CHAPTER 3

Danielle moped around the store all morning. Her dream the night before caused her to wake with an overwhelming sense of sorrow. She felt herself being dragged back down into confusion and grief. She needed a distraction. She needed Sawyer. She had to clear the air between them. She wouldn't apologize — she'd only drawn a picture, for God's sake — but she felt like she'd betrayed him. Their relationship needed to get back to its carefree beginnings. Maybe salsa at the Playa tonight would do the trick. She quickly taped a Be Back Soon sign on the screen and headed down the beach.

Danielle bounded up the stairs to Sawyer's apartment and rapped on the door. She anticipated Sawyer's easy-going smile on the other side. He should be back from surfing by now. The door opened, but instead of Sawyer, Desirée leaned in the doorway in only a towel. Her wet hair dripped onto her bare shoulders.

"Oh, hey. You're Danielle, right?" Her smile revealed perfect white teeth.

"Yeah, is Sawyer here?"

"He's in the shower. Do you want me to get him?"

Danielle's cheeks burned. "No, it's nothing important. I'll catch up with him later."

"Okay, I'll let him know you came by."

Danielle flew down the stairs. Angry tears threatened to spill over onto her cheeks. When she reached her house, she kept walking. Stupid, stupid girl. She should have expected this. They never spoke about being exclusive. She couldn't expect him to wait around for her. Danielle passed Noah's tent. She wondered if Kira had found him, and part of her hoped that she had. She was mad at the whole gender. She continued around the corner up to the ridge where the *flamboyán* trees grew. She paced, then picked up a rock and hurled it into the ocean.

"Stupid, fucking Sawyer," she yelled as she threw another rock. "And Desirée with your big tits. No, I don't want you to get Sawyer after you've fucked him." Danielle continued to hurl expletives along with the rocks.

"Wow, you're pissed."

Noah walked up the other side of the ridge, a camera slung around his neck.

"Great. Just the person I wanted to see. Go away before your fiancée Kira comes to beat me up." Danielle held a rock in her hand.

"First a lamp, now a rock," Noah mumbled to the ground.

"What was that? A lamp? Wipe that smile off your face or I'll knock it off."

Noah laughed. "You couldn't hit me if you tried. Your aim and your temper are horrible."

"Why do you act like you know me? You don't know anything about me and I don't want to know you. Please leave me alone."

Noah sat down and swung his legs hung over the edge of the ridge. He patted the ground next to him, then aimed his camera at the horizon.

Danielle gripped the rock. Tears blurred her vision. Her eyes focused on the wing tattoo on Noah's neck. It would be the perfect spot to aim for. But while part of her wanted to push him off the cliff, the other part imagined wrapping her arms around him, kissing him. She shook her head to erase the image.

"Listening to the ocean is soothing. It always helps me take my mind off my problems."

"You're ridiculous." Against her better judgement, she dropped the rock and sat next to him.

The waves crashed on the jagged rocks below the ridge. Brown pelicans flew past while clouds sailed across the sky.

Noah leaned back, his arm behind her. She was acutely aware of his body so close to hers. She inhaled the warm, salt air that ruffled through her hair.

"I heard Kira came by your shop. I'm sorry about that. We talked and she's on her way back to Fairview."

"It's none of my business. I don't know why she thought we knew each other."

Noah cleared his throat. "We're both from Fairview. When she found out I came here, she must have jumped to conclusions."

Danielle drew her legs up to her chest and rested her head on her knees. "It still doesn't make any sense. She said you worked construction."

"Poor Noah needed to support Kira's expensive taste. I mean I...I had to make money, but photography is what I love."

Danielle peered at him from the corner of her eye.

Noah pulled on one of her blonde curls.

"I like your hair longer. It looks nice this way."

Danielle swatted his hand away. "Longer? You say some strange things, Noah Hunt."

"Come on, come with me."

Noah stood with his hand extended. She hesitated, then took a deep breath and put her hand in his. He led her down a steep, narrow path on the other side of the ridge.

"Exactly where are we going?"

"Trust me." Noah smiled.

Why did she trust him? Her protective radar should be on high alert. Don't walk off with a man you hardly know, stranger danger and all that. But for some reason she felt safe with Noah.

The path leveled out and opened into a clearing that contained a large fenced-in area with palomino horses. Danielle had seen tourists on horseback-riding trips on the beach. This must be the ranch where they came from.

"Are you up for a little adventure?" Noah's eyes twinkled as he opened the gate.

"What are you doing? Isn't this trespassing?"

"José is cool with it. I'm going to take pictures for him when he leads groups on rides. He told me I could ride whenever I wanted to."

"I don't think he meant for you to come in and steal a horse."

"Give me a minute. I'll be right back." He strode across the paddock to the barn at the back of the property.

She could leave now. She should leave now. Go back to her apartment. It would be the right thing to do, the smart thing.

Noah led an enormous horse out of the barn.

"Danielle, meet Monster." Noah patted his mane.

"You're crazy. There's no way I'm getting on that horse."

"He's as gentle as a lamb. Come on. Grab the block. I'll give you a hand up. I promise you're going to like it."

"I know I'm going to regret this."

Danielle grabbed the block by the fence. Noah placed it next to Monster and held out his hand. "Step up and jump on."

"There's no saddle."

"No saddle if we're riding tandem."

Sweat trickled down the side of her face. The idea of Noah that close to her caused her heart to race. She pulled herself up over the back of the horse and gripped Monster's mane to steady herself.

"Relax." Noah swung up behind her. He grabbed the reins with one hand and wrapped the other around her. His chest pressed against her, strong and solid. His lips grazed her ear as he whispered, "Don't worry. We'll take it slow."

Noah clucked, and Monster plodded steadily down the path. They wound their way through the woods in silence. As their bodies rocked with the rhythm of the horse, every part of her that he touched tingled. The smell of his aftershave mingled with the faint scent of oil from his bike intoxicated her. But more than the physical attraction, with this stranger, she inexplicably felt at home. She leaned back into his chest and relaxed into the sway of Monster's gait. The trees thinned, and the trail opened into a small, secluded cove. Rock cliffs rose up on either side, protecting a perfect crescent of golden sand.

"It's so beautiful." Danielle murmured.

"I knew you'd like it." Noah slipped off the horse and helped Danielle down. He tied the reins to a branch at the edge of the woods, then joined her by the water. Danielle combed the beach for sea glass and shells while Noah snapped pictures of the gently rolling waves.

"Look at all this sea glass. It's the sea glass capital of the world. José has a nice little set-up here."

"Yeah, he's a great guy. The photography work I'll be doing for him is a big help. Smile for the camera."

Danielle stuck out her tongue, then couldn't help but smile as he clicked away.

"Can I ask you something?" Noah pointed his camera out over the water, his back to Danielle.

"Sure."

"That guy Sawyer, is he your...boyfriend?" Noah hesitated on the last word. "Is that who you were mad at?"

Danielle traced her thumb over the smooth edges of the piece of seaglass in her hand. "He's my friend, boyfriend, I don't know. We're not exclusive. I'm not really sure." What was she saying? "It's actually none of your business."

"Yeah, you're right. I'm supposed to be taking your mind off your little tantrum."

"Little tantrum?" Danielle scowled. She put her collection of sea glass on the sand before scooping up a handful of water to throw at Noah.

"Hey, watch out for the camera. This is expensive equipment."

"You're scared, is that it?" Danielle taunted.

"You're the one who should be scared. You're in trouble now." Noah lifted the camera from around his neck and placed it on a piece of driftwood. "You need to cool down. Yeah, that's exactly what you need."

Danielle backed away. "Nope. I'm fine."

Noah continued toward her.

"Come on. I've got all my clothes on. Monster doesn't want a wet rider."

"Oh, I think he'd be fine with it." Noah lunged forward and scooped her up in his arms. Danielle squirmed.

"Noah, please don't." She was inches from his lips. If she moved a little closer, she would be able to kiss them.

Noah's eyes sparkled with mischief. "I would love to listen to you beg some more, but here goes nothing." As he launched her into the water Danielle grabbed his waist and yanked him on top of her. Her heart raced as he leaned in and gazed into her eyes. Before their lips touched, he rolled off into the water.

"We're in now, might as well go swimming." Noah pulled his t-shirt over his head, exposing his muscled torso. Danielle's eyes widened as he peeled off his wet jeans. He crumpled up both and threw them onto the beach.

As she treaded water, her shirt billowed around her like a tent. She couldn't help but stare at his rippling abs.

"See something you like?" Noah chuckled.

"No, I'm just swimming, looking at the ocean. Has anyone ever told you you're a little arrogant?"

"Only you." Noah floated on his back. "Looks like you've got your own personal flotation device there."

"You're not funny." Danielle paddled away from him, hindered by the excess fabric.

"You'll never be able to get away from the sharks that way."

"Sharks? There aren't sharks here, are there?"

"There are sharks everywhere. We're in their habitat, you know."

Danielle mulled it over. A bra was like a bikini top, right? Her back to Noah, she struggled to pull off her shirt, then squished it into a ball and threw it on the sand. She sank back into the water up to her neck. Her shorts were staying on. She ducked underneath the water. When she came up for air, Noah was there next to her.

"Much better. Now you'll at least have a fighting chance."

They floated in the water and stared out at the horizon. Occasionally the tide pushed them together. A wave rolled past, and Danielle drifted in front of Noah. The short distance between them was electrified. Her eyes locked on the wing tattoo on his neck.

"Danielle, can we talk?" His serious eyes searched her face. As if reading her mind, he reached out to touch the tattoo of the wing on her shoulder. The way he looked at her like she was the most important person in the world confused her. His gaze burned into her until she had to look away.

"Monster!" she shouted.

Noah's forehead scrunched in confusion. "I just want to talk."

"No, Monster. He's gone. Look!" Danielle pointed to the tree where the horse had been tied.

"Shit, I must not have tied it tight enough." Noah splashed out of the water, Danielle behind him. "Hopefully he followed the path back home." Noah scooped up the wet clothes, sandals, and camera from the beach and pulled Danielle along with him. "Come on, José will kill me if I lose his horse."

Danielle and Noah sprinted through the woods. When they arrived breathless at the paddock, Monster was chomping happily at his grain box inside the corral. He glanced up casually as if to say it was about time they got back.

"Thank God," Noah exhaled.

"I told you he didn't want two wet people on his back." Danielle crossed her arms. "Can I have my stuff? I should probably get home."

Noah opened the wad of clothes and sandals in his hand. "Here are your sandals. Your shirt must still be on the beach."

Crap, thought Danielle.

"I could go back for it if you want."

"No, that's okay. It was just an old shirt."

Noah closed the gate and latched it shut. "I'll walk you back."

"You don't have to do that."

"No, I want to. I'd like to."

Danielle blushed.

In silence they walked up the ridge and back along the beach.

"When we were at the cove, you said you wanted to talk. What did you want to talk about?"

Noah ran his hand over his hair in that same uncomfortable gesture she had seen the day he first came into her shop. "I, it's just..." His words trailed off as they approached his tent. "Just a second." He ducked inside the tent and emerged with a Harley Davidson shirt. He had also put on a pair of shorts.

"Thanks." Danielle pulled the shirt over her wet bra. "I don't think I've ever seen you in shorts."

"Yeah, I figured I better get with the program if I'm going to live here, right?"

"Are you? Going to stay?"

"Yeah, I kind of like it here." Noah reached for the front of the too-large shirt and tied it in a knot at her waist. "It looks good on you."

As they continued toward her apartment, Noah reached for her hand. Danielle didn't pull away. She couldn't deny that she was happy that he would be staying in Areto.

"Looks like someone is waiting for you."

Sawyer sat on the sand next to her door.

Danielle inhaled deeply.

"Will you be okay?"

"I'll be fine. Thanks for the horseback riding. Come by with your pictures or if you want to hang out or whatever," she rambled.

Noah touched her shoulder. "I'll always be here for you, always."

Danielle looked back at him as he walked away. Why did she feel like she knew him, that his words were memories?

"You're finally back." Sawyer pulled an elastic off his wrist and gathered his hair into a ponytail.

"I don't have anything to say to you." Danielle scowled down at him.

"I didn't sleep with Desirée."

"Yeah, right. She was naked in your apartment so you could discuss Shakespeare."

"Leisa always says if you're looking for cockroaches in the cereal, you're going to find cockroaches in the cereal."

She put her hands on her hips. "Desirée's the cockroach and you're the cereal?"

"Come on, Danielle. We surfed all day; she came over to take a shower. Nothing else happened."

"It doesn't matter. You can do whatever you want. We never discussed being exclusive."

"Is that what you're doing with motorcycle boy? You run off with him first chance you get?"

"I did not run off with him. I bumped into him when I was walking off my irritation."

"And then you happened to end up in his shirt? I assume the Harley shirt is his."

"We didn't do anything. You are frustrating the hell out of me, Sawyer Reed!" Danielle clenched her hands into fists.

"Well, the feeling is mutual. Why are you pushing me away? I thought we were getting closer, and the past few days I have no idea where your head is at." Sawyer scooped handfuls of sand to bury his feet.

"I'm not trying to push you away." Danielle gritted her teeth.

"Well, that's what it seems like."

"You know it's complicated. I'm still sorting through a lot of stuff."

"You're so wrapped up in your past, you can't see anything else. Do you think you're the only one that's ever had anything horrible happen to them?"

"Wow. This coming from Mr. Sunshine and Rainbows. And what would you know about pain or losing people that you love?"

"Just because I don't wallow in it doesn't mean I'm not hurting too. People deal with pain differently. That tattoo on my hip that you're always so curious about? It's for my younger brother who died of leukemia. Don't tell me I don't know about pain."

Danielle slumped next to Sawyer. "I'm sorry. I don't want to fight with you."

Sawyer kicked at the sand. "I'm sorry too. I didn't mean those things. But you need to stop living in the past. You'll never be happy if you can't let go of the bad things that happened to you."

Matt had told her the same thing, and Vanessa. Were they right?

Sawyer held both of her hands. "You know I like you a lot, don't you?"

Danielle peered into his warm, brown eyes. Sawyer had been her comfort since she'd arrived in Areto. She nodded.

"I'm going to a surf competition in Hawaii next month. Why don't you come with me?"

Danielle's eyes widened. "Go with you, to Hawaii? I don't know. I have the shop. That's a big trip."

"Don't you ever do something without overanalyzing it? It's just a surf competition, it's not like I'm asking you to have my love child."

"Very funny. I can't just take off like that without thinking about it. And who says I'd want to have a love child with you anyway?"

"It was a joke. Don't worry, I'm never having kids."

"Really? You don't ever want kids?"

"Nope. After what happened to my brother and watching how it destroyed my parents, there's no way. Kids wouldn't fit into my lifestyle anyway. What about you?"

Danielle braced herself for the onslaught of emotions that usually suffocated her after any mention of children. The dull ache of loss still pulsed in the recesses of her heart, but her head was clear.

"I think I do." Danielle surprised herself with this admission. She realized she was finally ready to begin thinking about her future.

"Well, I think we've had enough deep conversation for one night. Back to the trip. Do you need some help making your decision?" Sawyer traced his finger down the side of her neck and curved it around her breast.

Danielle sighed. "I think I'm better off on my own for this one."

Sawyer kissed her gently on the lips. "I'll be at the shop all day tomorrow. I hope you'll say yes."

Danielle paced on her porch and shuffled her tarot deck. The worn cards slid through her fingers in a moving meditation. She had a choice: go with Sawyer or get to know Noah better. Or, she could not deal with anything and run again. The waves crashed in rhythm with her footsteps on the cool tiles. She circled like an animal trapped in a cage.

"All right, who's first?" Danielle pulled a card from the deck. The Knight of Wands. Sawyer. Sexy and kind, he helped her through a horrible period in her life when she couldn't get past her own misery. She considered Sawyer's offer. If she said yes, she knew the trip would be uncomplicated and fun, just like Sawyer. But after their conversation, she didn't know if she could imagine the relationship lasting long-term.

"Next." Danielle shuffled and pulled out The Lovers. She immediately thought of Noah. Was he the change in path she was destined to take? Their day on the beach had been amazing. Beyond the fact that he was gorgeous, she felt an inexplicable connection with him. It was as if she had known him forever. The words he said, the way she felt when she was with him made her remember her brief but profound affair with Xavier.

"He always reminds me of Xavier," Danielle repeated. "Exactly!" She hit her head with her hand. "I'm attracted to him because he reminds me of Xavier. It's always been Xavier." She shut her eyes and the memories she had carefully locked away rushed out. The moment she saw his face hovering above her, the first time she touched his skin, his lips soft against hers. When they made love, it was as if she had met the other half of her soul. Why did she ever leave? It was a simple choice. In fact, there was no choice. Their love transcended time, space, even death. It had been a mistake to ignore her feelings for Xavier all this time.

She couldn't wait another minute. Danielle rushed back inside and opened her laptop. She booked the first flight she could back to Fairview.

CHAPTER 4

Danielle had a day to pack up her shop and tie up loose ends before she left.

She said her goodbyes to Leisa at the Playa and told Ramón she would continue to pay rent until she knew for sure if she would be back.

She took a deep breath before entering the surf shop. Sawyer stood at the cash register ringing up a customer. When he looked up, Danielle gestured that she would be outside. She walked to the side of the building where she had painted the mural. She ran her hand over the wall, remembering the pain that had guided each brush stroke.

"You're not coming, are you?" Sawyer leaned against the wall.

Danielle turned to face him. "How'd you know?"

"I could see it on your face. You were never very good at hiding your emotions."

"I'm so sorry, Sawyer. I just don't think it's going to work out for us. I'm going back to Fairview. You were right. I need to face my past before I can start moving forward.

I hope you know how much you've meant to me. I don't know what I would have done without you when I first got here."

Sawyer cleared his throat. "Will you be coming back to Areto?"

"I'm not sure. I'm going to hold onto the apartment and store for now, until I figure out what I'm doing."

"So, this is goodbye." Sawyer looked past her shoulder. "For now, right?"

Sawyer cupped her face in his hands and kissed her cheek. "I'm glad I met you, Danielle. I hope you find what you're looking for. When you come back, we'll have a drink at the Playa and make fun of all the customers."

Danielle threw her arms around him in an enormous hug. She whispered against his chest. "You'll always be my knight."

The only goodbye left was Noah. She would take a walk on the beach later today. If he happened to be around, she would let him know her plans.

Danielle was carrying a box of pictures to the back room when the screen door creaked.

"Sorry, we're closed," she shouted as she pushed the box to the back of a shelf. She returned to the front carrying another empty cardboard box to fill.

"What's going on? Are you moving to a new location?" Noah's forehead creased with concern.

"Hey, Noah. I was going to come find you later. I'm going to be leaving Areto for a little bit."

"Wait, no, you can't go. I brought the pictures. I thought I'd have more time." Noah held an envelope in his hands.

"Time for what?"

Noah strode toward her and threw the envelope on the counter.

"For this."

He grabbed her face and kissed her. It was a hungry, desperate kiss filled with longing. The box dropped, and her hands pressed against his chest. As her lips opened to him, flashes of Xavier streamed through her mind. She pulled away.

"Noah, I'm sorry. I'm in love with someone else."

"You're in love with someone else? But we…" Pain seared his face.

"I really enjoyed our day on the beach. If things were different…I would have liked to get to know you more. You're…a really nice guy."

"A really nice guy?" Noah coughed. "In love with someone else. Well, that changes things." He ran his hand over his hair.

"Be happy, Danielle." Noah's jaw clenched. His eyes filled before he hurried out the door.

Danielle fought the urge to follow him. Her eyes lit on the envelope he had left on the counter. She opened it and flipped through photographs from their day at the cove — the ocean, the sky, Monster, and her. When she saw herself through his lens, she looked beautiful. She looked happy. She turned to the door. Was this another in the long line of her mistakes? Her afternoon with Noah was the first time she had felt whole and at peace since she had left Xavier. Xavier. Danielle clutched the pictures to her chest. Xavier was her destiny.

"I'll be there soon," she whispered.

After a restless night of sleep, Danielle showered and retrieved her bag from the back of the closet to pack. Tucked in the bottom of her suitcase was the photograph of Xavier. It seemed a lifetime ago that she discovered it wedged in the wallboard of her attic.

When she finished packing, Danielle lugged her suitcase downstairs and through the front door. As she pulled the door shut, she spotted an envelope taped to the screen. She ripped it off and opened it.

Danielle,

From the moment I saw you, I loved you. I only ever wanted you to be happy. I'm going to be leaving Areto. I hope you find the love and family you have always been looking for with Sawyer. Hold a place in your heart for me.

I'll always love you.
X .- Noah

Her hands shook as she pulled out a second piece of paper. It was the sketch she had drawn of Xavier at her house in Fairview while they waited for his brother Caleb. His face, her green eyes inside his, his eyes — Noah's eyes. Noah's eyes? Why did he have this picture? Danielle breathed in ragged gasps. The thoughts she had pushed aside and ignored stormed out in violent waves. Questions exploded in her brain. X? Was it a kiss? Was it an X for Xavier? Was this why Noah reminded her of Xavier? Could it be? Did he find a way to her? Was that what happened in the accident?

Danielle crushed the picture and the letter in her fist and took off at a run. She needed to catch him before he left. She was panting when she got to the spot on the beach where his tent used to be. All that was left was a flattened patch of sand.

"Damn it!" Danielle caught her breath and continued up the beach to the cliff. The flowers of the *flamboyán* trees scattered over the rocks like burning embers. She scrabbled down the other side and sprinted to the farm.

When she got to the fence, José was feeding the horses. "*Hola*, Danielle, *qué tal?*"

Danielle could barely spit the words out as she grasped the fence posts for support. "Have you seen Noah?"

"No, Noah *salió ayer*. He said he was moving on. *Es una lástima*, really too bad. He was doing a great job with the pictures."

Left yesterday? Danielle rested her head against the fence and held the letter to her chest. Was it possible that she had lost Xavier again? Where would he go?

"*Estás bien? Necesitas algo?*" José called out.

"No, I'm okay. I don't need anything. I'm going to walk to the cove."

Danielle trudged through the woods. As she replayed each minute she'd spent with Noah, she felt as if she were traveling down a dark tunnel from which there would be no return. She remembered their ride on Monster, her body nestled against his, the words he said, and how he looked at her like she was the only person that mattered. Thoughts swirled in her mind. Could it have been Xavier all along? But how? And now he thought she didn't want him. Danielle's heart was being ripped out of her chest.

Without Noah, the cove no longer seemed magical. The sound of the waves crashing on the shore was not soothing, but angry. The rocks loomed up on either side, no longer protective but ominous and cold. She released the papers she clenched in her hand, and watched as the wind lifted them up and tumbled them down the beach. She picked up pieces of coral from the shore—pale bones washed up from a watery grave—and then threw them back into the ocean where they belonged. Her hands shook, and her breath became shallow as panic set in. How would she find him? Where would she go?

Danielle held her head in her hands so it wouldn't explode. She fought to keep the tears from coming; she knew once they started, they would not stop. Images of Xavier and Noah morphed together in a dizzy kaleidoscope.

"Danielle?"

Noah's deep, velvety voice. Now she was hallucinating. Was it her fate to be forever tormented by visions and dreams, real love always out of reach? Maybe the days of love she experienced with Xavier were all she would get. She could return to Fairview and her old job and decide what to do next. Maybe Noah would end up there. She opened her eyes, her decision made.

At the entrance to the woods, Noah stood. Lines of pain creased his face.

Danielle froze.

"Noah," she whispered.

His face was hard, unmoving.

"I forgot one of my cameras at the ranch. José told me you were here. I want you to know that I understand. You deserve to be happy. You don't need to feel sorry for me." He stared at the ground.

Danielle slowly stepped closer, afraid he was a vision that would suddenly disappear.

"Is it really you?" She reached up to touch his face, then pulled her hand away. "Tell me about the first night we met."

"You were sitting on the floor of the baby's room. I tried to comfort you and tell you everything was going to be all right. You attempted to smash my head in with a lamp. And then, as I recall, you ripped my clothes off and attacked me." He smiled sadly.

Danielle started to shake.

He continued. "Your favorite color is blue. You used to do yoga on the living room floor. You eat apples for breakfast. You saw me when no one else could. You set me free."

"But how? How did this happen?"

Xavier looked at her with hungry, hopeful eyes. "There was a terrible storm one night. A motorcyclist crashed in front of the house. He was dying. I saw his spirit leave and took a chance. I slipped into his body. I'm not exactly sure how. I knew I needed to find you, be with you. I told you that I would find a way. I kept my promise to you."

"My dream." Suddenly the pieces fell into place. An avalanche of memories slid from where she kept them carefully sealed away. Tears clouded her vision. She swayed as if she were drunk.

"Danielle, Danielle?" Noah called, but his voice echoed from far away as she crumpled to the ground.

When she came to, she lay on the sand in Noah's arms.

"Are you okay? You passed out."

"I still can't quite believe it's you."

Noah stared past her into the waves. "I know it's not what you were expecting. I'll walk you back to your apartment. And then I'll go."

Danielle gripped his arms. "What? Why would you leave? You can't leave."

His expression hardened. "You said you were in love with someone else. With Sawyer. I won't be the one to cause you any more pain after what you've been through."

Tears spilled uncontrollably down her face. "I did say I was in love, but I never said I was in love with Sawyer. I was going back to Fairview to find Xavier, to find you. I'm in love with you. It's always been you."

Danielle threw her arms around him and crushed his body against her own. Noah's lips found hers. Kissing him felt like the most beautiful kind of drowning. She tasted the salt of her tears as they flowed down her cheeks.

"Don't cry, please don't cry," Noah pleaded. "I'm never leaving you again."

As she looked into his eyes, she saw the truth of her undying love for him reflected. At that moment the sky opened. Rain pelted them.

Noah grabbed her hand. "Come on. Let's get out of the rain." They ran toward the cliffs at the edge of the cove and into a small cave. The rain formed a curtain between them and the rest of the world.

Danielle shivered in her wet clothes.

Noah pulled her towards him and kissed her gently. "We can take it slow. I know this is a lot to comprehend."

"It's you, but it's not you at the same time." She ran her hand over the wing tattoo on his neck. "I should never have left."

"We could never have a life the way I was. Now we can. We can have it all, a house full of kids if you want, a life together. I love you."

Danielle felt as if a shadow had been lifted from her soul. She was no longer a hostage to her past. She placed her hands on his chest. His heartbeat pounded beneath her fingertips. She wound her arms around his back and kissed him deeply. Her eyes closed and she melted against him. She thought back to Fairview. In their short time together, they had connected in a way she never imagined was possible. He might be in a new body, but this was Xavier who knew her and loved her for who she was.

She opened her eyes. "I don't want to take it slow. I want you. I want a family, a life with you. I want to be your wife."

Noah laughed. "Was that a proposal?"

Danielle considered. "Yes, I guess it was. What's your answer?"

"Of course it's yes. A thousand times, yes. But there is one important thing we need to talk about." Noah kissed her forehead, cheeks, and lips. "Are you saving yourself for the wedding night?"

"I think that ship has already sailed." Danielle trembled under his touch. Lightning flashed outside the cave as the rain continued to fall.

"Ah, yes. I do recall. In fact, I think I remember exactly what you like."

His fingertips grazed her arms as he peeled her wet shirt above her head and then removed his own. He deftly unsnapped her bra and let it fall to the ground. One hand cupped her breast while his thumb circled her nipple.

She tilted her head up to find his lips, his tongue gently probing hers. His other hand slid down her belly. His fingers found her wet folds and caressed back and forth. When his thumb slid into her, she gasped with pleasure.

As he pulsed slowly in and out, Noah bent his head down to tug at her nipple with his teeth. He whispered against her breast, "Tell me what you want."

Danielle smiled, remembering when he spoke those words to her back at the house in Fairview. "I want you." She lowered herself to her knees and pulled his swim shorts down. She caressed his hard manhood and swirled her tongue around its tip. "I need you inside me."

The desperation and longing of the past few months took over. They tore the remaining clothes off each other and ended up tangled together on the soft sand on the floor of the cave. A flood of sensations swept over Danielle as they explored each other's bodies. She wrapped her legs around him. He thrust into her and she drove her nails into his back. Her orgasm spread across her belly in a tidal wave of shudders as he came inside her.

Danielle lay in Noah's arms. Covered with sweat and sand, she had never been happier. The rain slowed to a gentle patter. She caressed Noah's chest, memorizing the curves, wanting to stay forever in this perfect moment.

"I wish you had told me it was you when you arrived in Areto."

Noah stroked her curls. "I was afraid that you would get scared and run away again. I thought if you got to know me, it would be easier, and then there was Sawyer. You two seemed pretty close. Do I need to be worried about competition?"

Danielle thought back to her time with Sawyer. He was a big part of her life in Areto. She hoped that they could remain friends.

"Sawyer is a good friend. I was in a really bad place when I got here. He helped me through that. But no, you're the only one that I want. You're stuck with me now."

Noah gently traced the line of the scar on her leg. "I'm sorry it wasn't me that helped you through that. You've changed a little too, you know. You're more sure of yourself, confident."

Danielle snuggled against his chest. "But I'm still a little confused about one thing."

"Only one thing? What's that?"

"What should I call you? Noah? Xavier?"

"Considering Xavier is officially dead, Noah would probably be the wise choice."

"But what about the real Noah Hunt? Doesn't he have a life back in Fairview? And Kira? You told me she was gone, but she doesn't seem like the kind of person who is easily deterred."

"From what I could gather, Noah was a bit of a loser. No one came to the hospital to visit except Kira, and she was more interested in playing the grieving fiancée. Honestly, I think she was a bit disappointed that I recovered. I told her she could keep the ring, and she was happy enough to go. I know she sensed something was different. I'm yours, Danielle Williams, if you want me, that is."

Danielle reached down between his legs. "Oh, I want you, Noah Hunt. In fact, I think I want you right now."

The sunlight warmed her face. She must have slept late. She heard the patter of footsteps up the stairs and opened her eyes.

A boy ran across the room, hopped up onto the bed, and jumped up and down. "Mommy, wake up. We're going to the beach. We've been waiting for you to get up." He snuggled against her.

She breathed in the scent of his dark curls.

"Caleb, I told you not to wake up Mom." Noah leaned against the doorway cradling a baby. He walked over to the bed and kissed her as the baby's tiny arms reached out to her. "A quick kiss, Matthew, then let's go. We'll meet you at the beach." Noah grabbed Caleb's hand. "Don't be long." Noah's smile lit up his face before he headed down the stairs.

Danielle woke. It was a beautiful dream. Was this how her life would be with Noah? They had come back to her apartment in the early morning hours when Danielle finally succumbed to exhaustion. She rolled over to embrace Noah, but her hands grasped only a tangle of sandy sheets. Danielle panicked. Was it all a dream? She threw the covers off and looked around the apartment. Empty. On the kitchen table she spotted a plastic cup with red *flamboyán* flowers tucked inside. Next to it was a note.

Dearest Danielle,

I could hardly bear to leave you this morning, but there are some things I need to take care of today. Meet me at the cove at sunset. I promise this will be the last time that I ever leave you.

All my love,
Noah

The cove at sunset? It would be impossible to wait that long. What could he be doing all day? Danielle checked her phone. It was later than she thought, almost noon. But how could she occupy herself for seven hours? She could kill some time unpacking her pictures and setting the shop back up, since they discussed staying in Areto. She also needed to make an important telephone call. Karen would probably think she was insane, but she deserved to know the whole story. She was her best friend and had always been there for her, especially after her miscarriages and Matt's murder.

Danielle picked up her box of tarot cards from the floor. She perched on the edge of her bed, shuffled the deck, and pulled out the Ten of Cups. The man and woman embraced under a blue sky, their two children dancing next to them, their home in the distance. Was her happily ever after finally in sight? Danielle grabbed her phone and found Karen in her contacts. She chewed her fingernails while she waited for her to pick up.

"Danielle! It's good to hear from you! How's everything in Areto?"

"It's been interesting. Do you have a couple hours? I have a story to tell you."

Her conversation with Karen didn't take as long as she thought it would. Oddly, Karen accepted her tale of Xavier and Noah without too much convincing. She thought Karen's first reaction would be to jump on a plane to check on her mental stability. Danielle fussed with her hair. It had taken multiple rounds of shampoo to get rid of all the sand. Danielle smiled as she remembered the reason. She gathered it back in a ponytail and then put it back down again before giving up. She even put on makeup to waste time. She paced around her apartment. At 6:30, she couldn't stand the wait any longer, so she grabbed her sunglasses and headed to the cove.

When she arrived at the ranch, her eyes widened in surprise. Karen leaned against the fence stroking Monster's mane.

"Oh my God, what are you doing here?" Danielle ran to her friend and embraced her.

"I wondered how long it would be before you showed up. You never did have much patience." Karen grinned from ear to ear.

"But what are you doing here?"

"Noah called me at about five this morning. At first, I wanted to contact the police, but he knew everything about you, and I mean everything. It's a crazy story, but he convinced me. I always knew you were a bit of a strange bird, but this takes the cake. I got on the first flight I could.

When I heard from you, I was already here hanging out with Monster. It was hard to seem surprised when I was on the phone with you. How was my acting?"

"Awful." Danielle smiled. "I wondered why you took it so well."

"But why didn't you tell me when this was happening with Xavier, with Noah?"

"I didn't think you'd believe me. I hardly believe it myself." Danielle shook her head. "I'm still not sure this is real. Why didn't you come to my apartment?"

"Noah asked me to help him out."

"Help him out? So, you guys are BFFs now? Where is Noah, by the way?"

"He's around." Karen beamed. "And I must say his new bod might be an upgrade. You two will have beautiful babi... I'm sorry, Danielle, I'm stupid. I know that's still a touchy subject."

"No, it's okay. I had an amazing dream this morning. We had two boys. Everything will work out. I know it."

"I'm so happy for you, you deserve it." Karen squeezed Danielle's hand. "But enough of this jabbering. We need to get you ready. I see that sadly you tried to put on makeup and did a horrible job as usual. Come into the barn and we'll fix you up."

Danielle's eyes narrowed. "Get me ready for what? What's going on?"

"It's a surprise. I can't ruin the surprise, can I? What kind of friend would I be?"

"The last time you surprised me, it involved my mother. Please tell me she's not here."

"I promise. No Marla sightings today, although she'll probably kill me when she finds out."

"Finds out what?"

Karen hesitated. "That I came here without her since we had so much fun together last time. Let's go."

Danielle turned her face back and forth in the cracked mirror in the barn's bathroom. "You're amazing. You even got rid of the dark circles under my eyes." Karen had performed magic with her makeup bag. Her green eyes stood out even more and she had managed to tame Danielle's unruly curls into soft waves.

"One more thing. You need to change out of those shorts. There's a dress hanging on the back of the door."

Danielle peeked behind the door. A white sundress hung on a hook.

Karen checked her phone. "Come on, hurry up. We're supposed to be there at 7:30."

"All right, bossy pants, I'm getting dressed."

Danielle emerged from the bathroom and Karen clapped her hands. "Perfect. You are positively glowing."

Danielle blushed. "Are we going to a party?"

Karen grabbed her hand. "Yes, as a matter of fact we are. Come on, we don't want to be late."

The dimming light through the leaves dappled the trail. About halfway to the cove, lanterns hung on the branches of the trees illuminated their path.

Karen stopped behind the base of a tree to pick up two bouquets of red roses. "The big one's for you."

Danielle looked at her white dress and her mouth hung open. "We're not going to a party."

"Not exactly." Karen tilted her head.

"But, we never made any plans."

"Noah wanted to surprise you. And conveniently, José not only owns a horse farm but he is also a judge. I guess he was able to pull some strings with the paperwork. Isn't this what you want? If not, say the word and I'll Runaway Bride it with you."

"Of course it's what I want. I just wasn't expecting it today. I have flipflops on!"

"You are beautiful. It's a beach wedding." Karen hooked her hand through Danielle's arm. "Let's go get your happily ever after."

As she approached the cove, Danielle's heart beat so fast she was afraid it would explode in her chest, her feet so heavy she could barely move forward. When the path opened to the beach, she gasped. Noah paced back and forth beneath a wooden arbor strung with white roses and twinkling lights. He wore a gray suit and red tie that was charmingly crooked. José stood beneath the arbor in a white guayabera shirt and khakis. The last of the sun blossomed at the edge of the sea. A bird took flight in the pink glow. José whispered and put a hand on Noah's shoulder. He faced the entrance of the cove and beamed when he saw Danielle.

Karen tugged her forward until they reached the arbor.

Noah held both of her hands and gazed into her eyes. "I didn't want to wait another minute to start our life together. Will you marry me?"

As Danielle looked into Noah's eyes, she realized she was ready. Everything in her past led to this one perfect moment. Her heart was finally whole.

Danielle leaned up to kiss Noah. "I've been waiting my whole life for you."

She was not just ready to face her future, but to open her heart to all of it — to her painful, wild, messy, glorious life. And through it all, she would have Noah by her side for as long as they lived…and maybe even after.

FROM THE AUTHOR

Thank you for reading *The Lovers*! If you enjoyed it, I would be thrilled if you would consider telling a friend or leaving a review. For updates and news about upcoming books, visit my website www.JDBrettonWriter.weebly.com, follow me on Twitter @JDBrettonWriter, find me on Facebook, or connect with me by email at BrettonJD@gmailcom. I'd love to hear from you!

J.D. Bretton